D1370668

Copyright © 2004 by Nord-Süd Verlag AG, Gossau Zürich, Switzerland
First published in the Netherlands under the title *Goed zo! Knap hoor!*
by De Vier Windstreken, an imprint of Nord-Süd Verlag AG, Gossau Zürich, Switzerland.
English translation copyright © 2004 by North-South Books Inc., New York

First published in the United States, Great Britain, Canada, Australia, and New Zealand in 2004
by North-South Books, an imprint of Nord-Süd Verlag AG, Gossau Zürich, Switzerland.

Distributed in the United States by North-South Books Inc., New York.

Library of Congress Cataloging-in-Publication Data is available.
A CIP catalogue record for this book is available from The British Library.
ISBN 0-7358-1915-7 (TRADE EDITION)
1 3 5 7 9 HC 10 8 6 4 2
ISBN 0-7358-1916-5 (LIBRARY EDITION)
1 3 5 7 9 LE 10 8 6 4 2
Printed in Belgium

For more information about our books, and the authors and artists
who create them, visit our web site: www.northsouth.com

Nannie Kuiper

Bravo, Brave Beavers!

ILLUSTRATIONS BY Jeska Verstegen

Translated by J. Alison James

North-South Books · New York · London

Father and Mother Beaver sat on top of their lodge.
The logs that held the lodge together were a little
loose, and kept slipping, but Father and Mother were
having so much fun watching their children, they
didn't do anything about it.

Ben said to Becky, "Let's show them what we can do!"

Ben stayed under the water
for a long time.

Becky swam all the way to the other bank
before Ben came back up.

  Mother and Father Beaver cheered. "Bravo!"

All day long the beavers played happily.

It was late in the afternoon when Father
Beaver first noticed the storm clouds.
"Come! Come quickly!" he called.

The beavers rushed to the bank.

Father said, "It looks like a bad storm is coming. If the wind blows too hard, it could smash our lodge to pieces. We have to make it stronger!"

Mother gnawed down branches as fast as she could. Becky dragged them to the lodge. Father held them while Ben packed in mud to keep them in place.

The storm grew closer. The wind wailed, and rain pelted down.
"I think that should hold it!" said Father. "But maybe we should add a few more logs, just to be sure."

Mother said to Becky, "There are no more trees the right size here. We'll have to go into the forest!"

Becky was worried.
There were wild animals
in the forest, and she
couldn't escape them there
by diving underwater.

The wind howled. The trees bent
and swayed, creaking loudly.
"Watch out!" Mother shouted.

Too late! With a loud crash, a tree
toppled, landing right on Becky's tail.

"Ow!" cried Becky. "My tail! I'm stuck!"

Mother tried to move the tree, but it was just too big. "I'll have to get help," she said. "I'll be right back."

The storm was as loud as a waterfall—
too loud to hear any wild animals
approaching. Becky trembled with fear.

The river roared. Ben and Father swam for their lives.

"That mud washed right out of my hands," Ben shouted to Father.

"Just get to shore," Father said.

Mother stood at the shore. "Hurry!" she cried. "Becky is stuck. We have to rescue her!"

When they got to the fallen tree, they couldn't see Becky.

"Becky!" they called.

A pile of leaves rustled, and Becky appeared. "I was hiding from the wild animals," she said.

"Bravo!" said Father.

Together, Father, Mother, and Ben were able to lift the giant tree just enough for Becky to slip her tail out.

The storm was so wild by then that the river looked more dangerous than the land. The beaver family decided to spend the night in the forest. They burrowed under the leaves, just as Becky had, and snuggled together.

In the morning, the storm was gone. The birds were singing, and the sun was warming their bed of leaves.

Father stood up, shaking his fur clean. "Let's check on the lodge," he said.

"We did it!" cried Ben.
They had saved the lodge. Not a stick was out of place.
Bravo, brave beavers!